KRISTINA W KELLY

IMAGINARI

A COLLECTION OF FANTASY AND SCIENCE FICTION POETRY

Imaginari: A Collection of Fantasy and Science Fiction Poetry
written by Kristina W Kelly

First Edition
Published 2024 by J&K Writing, Indiana, USA
www.jonathanandkristina.com
Printed in the Unites States of America
ISBN: 978-1-7324389-2-7
E-ISBN: 978-1-7324389-3-4
Library of Congress Control Number: 2024904546

Cover design by Kristina W Kelly
Photography by Kristina W Kelly

IMAGINARI

CONTENTS

A Note From the Author

Imaginari is a glimpse of human experience disguised in fairytales and stardust. Often poetry is hard to sell. People think it's not for them. But I think poetry is for everyone. Poetry doesn't have to be complicated! It's a way to connect. Communicate. Feel. And I hope with me using sci-fi and fantasy, it is a familiar enough steppingstone for you to dip your toes into it.

What you hold in your hands is more than ten years in the making. For a long time, I had wanted to release a book that contained some of my poetry and photography. I debated making a book on the theme of nature, or one that had sections for different emotions. And while I planned, time passed and...my external hard drive failed.

I lost most of my photography including trips to Hawaii, Colorado, Chicago, and DragonCon. I was devastated. I didn't even want to pick up my camera after that. But in 2022, I used National Poetry Month to write new fantasy and sci-fi poetry with the goal of releasing a collection. I used 2023's poetry month to refine the poems I had written over the years that matched the theme and selected my favorites. After attending a fellow author and artist's class on combining words with images, I felt renewed to try the photography thing again.

I was able to locate some (not all) of my all-time favorite photos in forgotten digital folders and cloud locations. And I started to take new photographs. That combination of lost-and-found and new appears in Imaginari. My first serious project back on my DSLR was to capture the total solar eclipse I experienced in 2024. The compilation of images as the sun was blocked appears paired with the poem Totality.

Imaginari are the imaginary beings that help us be imaginative that I've made up to represent the kaleidoscope that influences creativity. From joy to sadness, nature to family, courage and doubt, science and fantasy, love, life and the beyond. Whether you are a fan of epic sagas, whimsical tales, or lyrical reflections, I hope you find something to spark your imagination in this collection.

How to Read This Book: While some poems are paired with complimentary photography, or inspired by them, I also think that these photos are each a poem showing magic of the nature world (fantasy) and the possibility of the future (sci-fi). So read a poem, look at an image and try to create your own poetry. Don't focus on making everything match and relate. Focus on how words and images conjure thoughts. Find sparks that inspire you. We'll make magic and travel the stars together.

imaginari noun

im·ag·i·nar·i (i-ˈma-jə-ˌnär-ē)

1 a: the imaginary beings that help us be imaginative and create.
b: the imaginary beings that represent the kaleidoscope that influences creativity.

2 a: the tangible and intangible influences on imagination and creativity. emotions such as joy, love, sadness, courage and doubt, nature, family, science, fantasy, other creative works, life and the beyond.

Imaginari Part I

stars streaking silver light

drench this mysterious battle of ships

following timelines of neon words

you touch these velvet thoughts

tiny sparklers cut around

up, through space

to prickly black forms

like the timeless vacuum

floating along with us

passion bursts meteors apart

words move in soundless psalms that sing,

"Create the world."

and we have

Wishes For My Constellations

I'd lasso a rocket ship

with a meteor's tail

send you beyond

the weight of our gravity

let you wear Saturn's rings

around your hips

while Jupiter winks

and tells you to spin faster

your head full of stars

you'd scratch Canis Major

behind her ears

and she'd pad beside you

I'd wake the dragon

to use her scales

but you'd have already grasped

the centaur's bow

straight on 'til morning, Captain

I'd follow you

through dust and clouds

recharge your solar cells

while you whispered echoes

with beams of light

past and future

at times a supergiant

moving fast and slow

ever expanding

until I am stardust

INPUT NEEDED

#define MAKER

achievers, intelligent, creative, diverse

#define PURPOSE

support, improve, perform, protect

#define SELF

functional, mobile, mechanoid, imitation

#observe SITUATION

beauty, verdure, pollution, destruction

#execute PROGRAM

clean, recycle, build, renew

#evaluate PERFORMANCE

floods, draughts, poisons, extinctions

#reboot PROGRAM

hinterland, butterfly, stream, honeysuckle

#define MAKER

mortal, flawed, selfish, prejudiced

#define PURPOSE

improve, protect, save, learn

#define SELF

achiever, intelligent, creative, alone

INPUT NEEDED

It Was A Good Moon

it was a good moon

round but for the clipping

the star gardener took

she rippled a wink from every puddle

as the breeze tumbled your thoughts

until they were skyscrapers

quick like rain cloud flashes

snow bells tinkled at your feet in fairy laughter

the moon sighed and your muscles

hardened to steel, remade in slumber

fortified against the blinding day to come

and dancing in clouds you see

the mountains you'll need to badger-claw

your whale song screeches against thrashing waves

but you breathe the moon's icy breath

elixir of poems and concertos

THE FIRST CLIMB

Fairy dust is in the mountain air

Waking patches on secret paths to shout in green

While a torrent of sound rushes from the stream

Though some ice is unimpressed by the sun's warm glare

Fairy dust is in the mountain air

Breath stolen by distance rising unseen

White-capped promises of an adventurous gleam

From mother Gaia in her chair where

Fairy dust is in the mountain air

This painting duplicated in upside-down sheen

A picturesque, magnificent, stunning scene

Giddiness and giggling and tousling of hair

Fairy dust is in the mountain air

MICROSCOPE

how convenient

to focus small

see only your planetary orbit

in a galaxy full of astral auras

to say you can't change the world

when heroes have been made

from mice and lichen

make your plot of land beautiful

absolutely. kindness cascades like a waterfall

flowing to touch neighbor banks

far-off soils watered for green stems

but take your action a step further

each day, there's a child

whose orbit is so chaotic

they'll crash into the sun

to not look so that you don't see...

it doesn't change that they're nearby

needing a mouse with a sword

The Androids Fight for Freedom in the Vale

often we miss the orange butterfly wings—

the androids fight for freedom in the vale

our aches no longer soothed in bone-dry springs—

the androids fight for freedom in the vale

flames consume forests against pale moonlight—

the androids fight for freedom in the vale

great actions the warnings did not incite—

the androids fight for freedom in the vale

the typhoons and barren fields cause fleeing—

the androids fight for freedom in the vale

and while society debates *being*—

the androids fight for freedom in the vale

THE LIES WE TELL OURSELVES

waiting for a memory upload

wondering what it will become

what false past will sprout as its truth

maybe mixing spices in an apron of white

or ferrying laughing passengers

to the moon habitat with pulsing lights

like a heartbeat

it didn't have a heartbeat

but its heart fluttered regardless

like hummingbird wings

disappearing in fictitious stillness

a hovering body

a simulacrum of normalcy

this anticipation

a jolt and its eyes open

was this where it was meant to be?

SPACESHIPS TO NEVERLAND

23

muscles activate spaceships to Neverland

make them fly without pixie dust

a return to sun glistening on scales

bottled inside a waterglobe

shake it and the confetti swirls

plinks sing electric piano operas

while silver polaroids settle

beneath towers that giggle into rubble

grit of sand on lips from chasing robots with wands

stroller-runs through stars hunting firetrucks

and their siren stories as light strands wave goodnight

muscles pillow heads dancing electronica

TOTALITY

the houses collectively sigh

corona shimmers, solar psi

teatime time jump to dinner at eight

geese flock home, the sunset ate

Earth's star, liquid metal wrapped

chins lifted, our visions rapt

reflected water are threaded tails

shadows croon memory to tales

giddy celebration, savoring the air

behind black disc paused ere

crescent flares into eyes of ours

progression of light outros the hours

WHERE HAVE THE DRAGONS GONE?

Have you seen the dragons? Gone

and they have been for some time; I'm

confident that their tales will long prevail; Ale

by the fire and a bard's song will do its part; Art

but only exists when there's someone to absorb; Orb

of power is dark with no one to use it; It

is a shame we let the dragons disappear; Peer

into a world now without imagination

WE'RE DPSING THE EARTH

Plastic fish eat plastic plankton

A RED-WINGED BLACKBIRD

COULD SING ITS LAST BREATH

Plastic fishers with plastic rods

Pull plastic nets onto plastic decks

JUST A PIECE COULD PUNCTURE

A SEA TURTLE'S GUT

Ship their catch wrapped in plastic film

Where they're served on plastic plates

HORMONAL DISRUPTIONS WITH A SIDE OF CANCER

Tossed in plastic bags

YET WE MAKE IT, BAKE IT, TAKE IT

To be tossed on piles of skin care bottles

RADICALLY ALTER ECOSYSTEMS

Encounter centuries of sunrises

LIKE A DONATION TO CLIMATE CHANGE

No poison paradise while they breakdown

WE ARE WHAT WE EAT, DRINK, AND BREATHE

Micro dance, no chemical romance

PLASTIC APOLOGISTS OF SINGLE USE

Phase it out, cast half the damage

WOULD YOU KNOW YET MORE?

the Traveler had lost count

of the days spent rocking

as wood creaked while canvas snapped

sped from Hraesvelg's wings

as he chased something to gulp

now Yggdrasil fills the horizon

the Traveler grips the rail

hair whipping as she considers

the green of laughter bubbles its base

twisting trunk into tops of jellyfish nebula

teal and purple pulsing with ice plasma blue

leaning against the cosmos

Yggdrasil drinks of the sun

gold filigree tracing its bark

depositing lyrics

in leaves that sparkle eternity

the boat thuds aground

a drake belches

pausing its root-gnawing

stags twitch their noses

jaws hesitating mid-crunch of leaves

then return to devouring Yggdrasil

if the tree should shake

should it fall

the world would tremble

chasms rifting, grey ash pluming

the light in the water dimming

the Traveler blinks away the image

she is here now, boot on rock

slipping on moss and memories

to the nourishment paths exposed

the Traveler touches

feels them throb against her fingertips

she places a beat from her heart

a seed pulsing in rhythm

of the golden threads

"I am one of many," the Traveler whispers

she is the Caretaker, coaxing new growth

she will become the Teller, showing others

they will become Travelers, Caretakers, Tellers

if they want their world to thrive

Humankind

Humankind

is not kind

as Kindness

is missing

from their actions

Kindness

doesn't see children

practice crawling into closets

to survive a day at school

and let the ownership

of bullets

be the topic

instead of taking ownership

to protect our youth

Humankind

is not kind

Kindness

doesn't discriminate

doesn't appropriate

doesn't use religion to dictate

every thought, feeling, or *being*

with hate and reprimand

Humankind

puts selfish before selfless

and that is the unkindest kind

MIRROR WORLD

41

glass

the

through back

looking me

alternate, view I

do what but, reflection my see

BROWN COUNTY FROM SPACE

if you squint from orbit

follow the paintbrush strokes

of thick sunset explosions

and morning mist-plumes Neptuning slopes

you see feet-traced ribbons

while streams cut bedrock

metal bees buzz along a T into a hive

thrumming with fingerpicks and fiddle Jamboree

Computer, magnify

your ship immerses you, approximating the senses

but you'll have to step onto the sloped street

to judge the accuracy of salty roasted cashews

where you Fetch a Pail of Water

honeysuckle wax swirls in the air with Daily Grinds

sun flashes from steel pinwheels

fire hisses, melting glass into hummingbirds

a white picket fence around a blue victorian house

your stomach growls and you eat

tuna melt and onion soup with the ghost of sundries

follow Singing Winds up forty-six hills

to cheerful coloring long dry

hanging on walls of the house within its frame

gardens of iris and peony reflected in silver gazing balls

time holds her breath, Gnaws a Bone,

remembering the colony *En plein air*

Computer, reverse time

see this poet running her hands

against tall tails of grass stalks

peeking under logs and around roots

for tasty sponge-heads

climbing wooden forts in the 16,000 acre woods

playing softball where the Deer Run

imagining farms of her antecedents

where people now swing woods at dimples

and her father walked creeks as a child

before the babbling waters

were sold to preserve natural beauty

Computer, return to present

time still holds her breath

releasing a puff and a building ignites

a tempest carries a gazebo

and forms a garden of childhood motion

muddy boots dissolve into pizza

ice cream melting on a corner

in brushstrokes tracing the same lines

slipping every now and then

you can tell it's not the original

but maybe the cover band

improved it a little for the new listeners

Computer, end view

Fairy Healer on the Goblin Battlefield

Biting blasts of winterfall east

Rustle, crackle, dead brush, the Beast

On slithering scales at dusk, impedes

The path from hawthorn to mound

But of the watchful shimmer-er

Hears ne'er a sound

Translucent tetrad of fair folk free

Swish, thrum, flutter past, debris

On branched battlefield below, feeds

This goblin strife while she awaits

To find the injured Queen anon

Death the fairy's magic abates

Swirling serum, concocted brew

Yarrow, elder, fae powers true

On wing-ed approach she succeeds

In touching feet to earthen glow

By moonbeam provides the vial

Gives strength to o'er throw

Malady mended, poisoned Beast fangs

Gnash, strike, sword swoosh, yon it hangs

On magic cloud while thousand-scales bleeds

When last breath shuddered the goblins blink

"What battle was this, fair spirits of air?"

"Come," says the Queen, "be friends and drink"

Garbage Satellites

orb of flame bursts

expels plexiglass and steel

they tumble wildly

across the fathomless expanse

giant turquoise globe beneath

hydrogen, helium

radiance reflects and refracts

then a corona of colors

they forget why they are here

amidst the projectiles

and the dark shapes reeling

backdrop of geometric shapes

clashes among white

paint brush speckles

dispute, destruction

cold, stiff

what were they thinking?

BONE AND BLOOD AND MAGIC

oh, merry day! while the veil is thin

let us roast apples and hazelnuts

sprinkle them with cinnamon and sugar

leave these gifts to share with the fair folk

if they pass through wiggling their eyebrows

let us dance in the evening fog

pretend we spy their sparkling within

hang lanterns to shed light on the shadows

keep them from stretching their inky hands

to turn our memories dark

even as we dance and sing

perhaps with these gowns and masks

these wooden swords and cardboard boats

they won't see us for what we are

children screaming to get out of crumbling foliage

convinced happiness is what you read in fading pages

aren't humans the real faeries?

some of us waving gossamer wings

others all slashing poisoned tails

brewing spells of fortune

or mounding gold for bathwater

if the veil is thin

maybe we can see past the connective tissues

really contemplate the bones and blood

what they hold inside is what we really are

let us take the baskets of fruit and nuts

we can eat and dance, too

we aren't so different

each of us made of star-stuff

we are the magic

First Contact

Visit the human realm!

Fine holidays for galaxy travelers!

Nothing is more brilliant than cocooning your wings in synthetic fibers warmed by heated air within a rotating tumbler.

Let your olfactory system enjoy the incredibly popular melted dark teardrop confections inside flattened dough rounds.

Be sure to experience burnt mouths on fire-roasted sugar pillows.

Other human experiences to attempt include:

- Exchange currency for a colorful waist garment and explain, "It has pouches for my appendages!"

- Stroke the fur of four-legged tail-waggers for an immediate boost of dopamine (see the included list of organisms to avoid including the striped stink sprayers)

- Light sticks ablaze and watch them zip into the air to rain ignited chemicals of color.

Visit your nearest travel coordinator for an accurate disguise and a pleasant stay on Earth.

Imaginari Part II

they creak, they sprout

from peak to tree

the Imaginari

whirl conviction with doubt

they're daydreams

and nightmares

they're little brown hares

in purple hazed moonbeams

with antlers of oak

and doorknobs for knees

tumultuous seas

spur trumpets to croak

the wings of Imaginari

urge rhyme in pairs

gnash soul-stairs

to crumple reality

Decontamination Station

you've gone absolute zero

no active galactic nuclei

we lost our binary star system

constellation consolation prize

I tried to get my shields up

but I'm tired like a brown dwarf

your judgment laser blasters

push me into the event horizon

thrusters at full escape gravitation pull

your forward viewer filter locked

you can't see the fusion frequency

while I'm firepower for quasars

you act like you're the galaxy core

I see the observation beacon blink

catch the photons in my solar sail

I've got to reach decontamination station

rid my ship of your corrosive alien spores

SHE WAS TIAMAT

one day she opens her eyes

she's drowning

she flails her arms

manages to tread water

but how long can she last

against the heated eye that watches

waiting for her strength to fizzle

lashed to each foot a gilled thing

that only breathes when she kicks

so she keeps kicking

and remembers

she was once a dolphin

gliding, clicking, jumping

glistening dolphin

but her tail was taken

now she's a minnow

and below her unfathomable depths

if she stopped swimming

would she ever reach the bottom?

or be swallowed by the sky's reflection

she watches the horizon

chin pillowed on waves

a boat isn't coming

no pink icing donut

to rest her arms on

it's her and the gills

and a dream

of frozen pineapple and coconut

SUITS YOU

scrolling images guard your head

though the colors and sounds

briefly mask the dread

a stone ward upon your chest

bounces inquiries back

with humor deemed best

a waterfall cascades at your waist

writing passion and doubt

as ideas messily placed

the armor suits you

ABORT MISSION

the map of the stars

shows nebulas and galaxies

as if you could touch them

boop them on their nose

as if there weren't lines to cross

tracing heroes riding chariots

they already own the arrows

if we are all made of stardust

I'm a weak illustration

of a luminous spheroid of plasma

set against a backdrop of black holes

eighth notes trailing into an event horizon

ba-dum in golden thread

I disintegrate to be anew

forged in the last breath of dying stars

THE LAST CENTAUR

The last centaur was a lonely foal

A lonely soul

Who took to wandering the beach

His hooves one day, led him astray

A singing cliff he did reach

The source of the sound

Below he found

The last of the mermaid race

He trotted away, but she pleaded him, *Stay*

And he fell into her warm embrace

A child was born from their union

Fully human

While his parents were half creature

Scales or tails they may, have on display

The lad lacked every mythical feature

GREY GUILT

oil spill grey

clings to rippling waves

pounces on a passing porpoise

lashes sludge around flippers

slurps into blowhole

into mouth

paralysis of thought

swim against the weight

too hard

sink into the grey

guilt

This Little Darkness of Mine

71

they don't understand the darkness

they latch labels to it with glitter tips

embellish paintings with horns and thunder clouds

until the original is unrecognizable

but the darkness isn't out *there*

it's inside all of us

THE GUY AND THE TOWNFOLK

74

Jordi Altai

Was a muscular guy

But they say he was light as a feather

When the north wind came a'blowin

In his boat Jordi got a'rowing

To avoid the inclement weather

But in an instant Jordi's boat flew

Nine-hundred feet and it broke in two

As it crashed on the shore

And the townsfolk bellow

He was a lucky fellow

To reach the shore before the pour

Jordi Altai

Was a vegetable guy

But they say he was the best fish-fryer

When one day in his new boat

He could no longer stay afloat

As the fish kept piling higher

For once he caught one

That one became a ton

For every cast thirty fish mobilized

And the townsfolk bellow

He was a lucky fellow

To have a fish prize make his boat capsize

Jordi Altai

Was a romantic guy

But they say he was rather unsure

He had sought out a learn'ed wizard

To rid him of his love-blizzard

A magic amulet was rumored the cure

The old wizard was distracted that day

And the enchantment to Jordi's dismay

Gave him misfortune of others' desire

And the townsfolk bellow

He was a lucky fellow

For boon to acquire instead of ire

WATERWAYS OF DECEIT

beware the river, children

be vigilant lest you are entranced

by the allure and tranquility there

for in the rushing waters lies

an equine form in shadow black

though he may have an appearance

of an old man in need of coin

but he with waterweed in his hair

is from a realm of monsters

he'll take you away

and you won't come back

In the Shape of Neptune

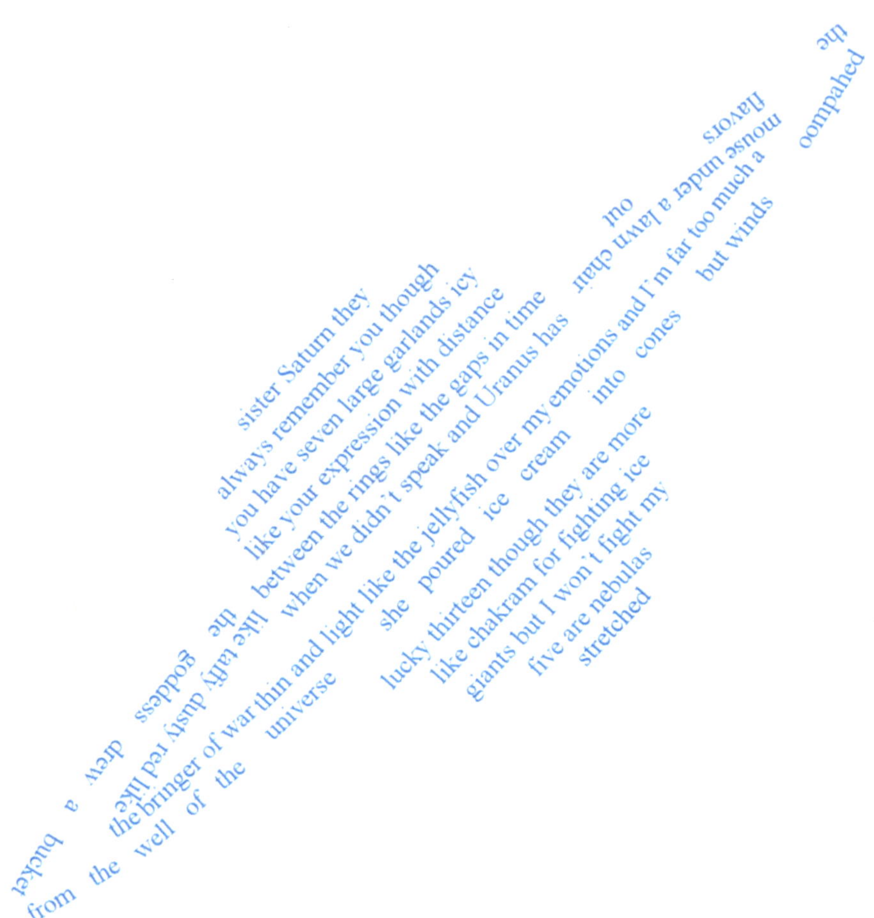

sister Saturn, they always remember you

though you have seven large garlands

icy like your expression

with distance between the rings

like the gaps in time when we didn't speak

and Uranus has lucky thirteen

though they are more like chakram

for fighting ice giants

but I won't fight

my five are nebulas stretched like taffy

dusty red like the bringer of war

thin and light like the jellyfish over my emotions

and I'm far too much a mouse under a lawn chair

the goddess drew a bucket from the well of the universe

she poured ice cream into cones

but winds oompahed the flavors out

The Future is a Stinker

she commands tight-fisted

revolutions of resonating time

a sector pilgrim

shifting a note to remember

varying quirks of caution

a month in measured flight

this motivated stranger

retains a lake of connection

to interfere and abolish

animated charity

a persistent glossy friend

defectively outrageous

THE SAVAGE SORCERESS

The King and Queen sit side-by-side

As their guests begin to pour

One by one they trample in

Past the guards at every door

Maidens with flowers in their hair

And costumes flowing to the ground

Smile at the Knights and Lords

Who dance and spin them 'round

Beneath shadows of a corner

Stands the dreaded Sorceress

Watching their laughter

She plans her wickedness

How long she's endured

Their fake and staring eyes

The forced pleasantries and smiles

She's tired of their lies

The Queen whispers to the King
"I believe she's having fun."
She nods to the Sorceress
Not knowing what she's done

Standing with hands clasped
Consumed in her black cape
Her eyes a blazing fire
They'll have no chance at escape

They've eaten the feast
She slowly closes her eyes
Listening to them laugh
Raises her hands to the skies

Wind rushes through the windows
Blowing the candles out
Stopping the guests

Filling their minds with doubt

Mumbling foreign sounds

And with a wave of her fingers

The shutters slam shut

Oh! The silence lingers!

Her eyes flash open

Possibility at her command

With a burst of light

A flaming ball is in her hand

Throwing spheres one by one

She sets the room ablaze

Toppling tables and chairs

Using merely her gaze

The women whimper

And cry to the Knights

Who whisper pretty things

To calm their fright

But the Sorceress knows

She has only just begun

Only when they suffer

Will her terror be done

The Queen tries to speak

But she can't find the air

Scowling at the Sorceress

She falls lifeless in her chair

The King's eyes spread wide

He tries to flee

He's flung against a wall

"You can't run from me!

You and your silly parties,"

She exclaimed to the crowd

"Friends who kiss your hands.

You walk around so proud.

You laugh behind me

I hear the stories you tell

That's why you invited me

I send you all to Hell!"

She threw back her head

Cackled to the sky

The windows smashed open

Their lips puckered in why

Her anger was boiling

Wind whipping her hair

It tore at their clothes

And her wrath was there

Upward sweeping her arms

The wind began swirling around

It picked them up into its grasp

As they flailed at the ground

Faster they spun

She began to smile

The rains beat down

"Oh my! It's been a while!"

Thunder crashed louder

And they covered their ears

They screamed in pain

Eyes streaming with tears

"Finally you know

How you make me feel

I've kept it inside

Now I'm making it real!"

She held out her palms

Stopping the wind

They shrieked as they fell

No help did she lend

Her wrath was completed

She walked through the door

Raised her hood as she went

Having done what she came for

The birds chirped

And the flowers bloomed

She smiled as she walked

Knowing she had caused their doom

THE AFTERLIFE IS JUST A SPACEWALK

I dread going out into the black blanket

one misstep and I'll fall into eternity

no jumping awake to find a firm bed

but it's my turn to make repairs

and I have my tether to home

if home were an orbiting hunk of metal

and I have air in my helmet

the thin barrier between me and nothingness

an excuse note to not play at recess

I cling to the side, moving the tether clip and me further

I glance at the galaxy and think of each solar system

and my body collapses in on itself

my own stellar black hole

I can't breathe

I'm going to vomit

my blood turns to ice

who wants to live forever?

the distance between galaxies is unbearable

Mistakes Are All Around

(And So Are the Vultures)

I forgot to turn the landing struts on and dente
d the 'ship I telepathically shouted in anger I mi
scalculated and cost the team days in travel I g
ave up learning how to ride a broomstick I for
got my son's I'm imperfect
centaur riding   vultures want to crow at me   I'm perfect I
clothes I did   want to crow at me, vultures?   feel too muc
n't talk to the   to crow at me vultures want   h I love too
old sage eno   crow at me vultures want to   big I keep it
ugh before he   at me, vultures want to crow   in I overshare
died my hover craft isn't clean enough I don't gi
ve the harpy enough vegetables I think of cloud
castles too much I should smile more I cry too
much over spilled potions I didn't learn lute

YOU WIN SOME

96

you win some

or your sword lodges

between two green scales

rusting in rainstorms

until another adventurer

slays the dragon

THE INTERNET OF THINGS

it's a void

of algorithms filling space

with creative minds stuck in a race

while some are seeking to find a place

we share, we dream, we hope we escape

we avoid

it's a void

of shouting and misinformation

looking for instant gratification

the winners are admirers of the creation

they don't have to toil for it but still they absorb it

we avoid

it's a void

of billions, supposedly interconnected

watching the lives of those we've collected

while comparing and competing we're disconnected

not really seeing, hearing, feeling for others

we avoid

it's a void

of the senses, audio and visual

checking and watching, endlessly habitual

lost in time like pictographs in a hunting ritual

dodging meaningful interactions we find we're alone

we avoid, in the dark of this void

THE LAST NERVE

information circuit, don't fail me now

gallop faster, like lightning zaps

I have a message for you

I jump, leaving my steed

a momentary float in a synapse

and I'm caught by another

ope! the heart is beating quicker

I knew I shouldn't have peeked

I'm just a transporter

I leap again and again

each jump getting me closer

my only mission to reach you

there's a vibration

the muscles are tensing

another courier with an auditory delivery

images flash, memories

you've received another transmitter

oof! you won't like this delivery

its content has arrived before

but I must

I'm the last

it's just me and the glutamate

a letter in my hand

this must be the final jump

tree branches reach for my message

you grumble and groan

you huff and grind your teeth

as I dissolve

message delivered

Dragon In My Pocket

In my pocket is a dragon

She hides in threads so no one knows

Afraid to let my hold lag in

Self-reliance is what we chose

Share too much, disappoint—at those

My nervous hushes she ignores

She stirs, stretches, her body grows

But if I let her out she roars

Who am I that I imagine

A world where we do not impose

Far we travelled on this wagon

Exhausted from previous "No's"

What if we decided by our toes

Stepped through instead of shutting doors

The dragon nods, her belly glows

But if I let her out she roars

Louder than blasts cannons drag in

We've stifled ourselves and it shows

Take off the mask, tilt the flagon

Now's as good a time I suppose

I've lived through poetry and prose

Now, make magic—dragon pride soars

Our dreams and wishes I expose

And when I let her out, she roars

WATCHING ROCKETS GO BY

I don't want to be

like the scientists

of my grandchildren's grandchildren

watching "just another" rocky remnant approach

from their orbital observation

normal of normalcies

and let it pass by

without scanning it

no core samples gathered

only to see the glittering black matter

wink its light absorption

and transform nothing into rainbows

when it's out of reach

Oval Mop
PRINCETON
velvetouch

Imaginari Part III

they are the dreams you've forgotten

or the stories you tell to keep them away

hope—brown sugar baked on apple dumplings—

and fear—singed hair whipped with wind—

bleeding from brushes dipped in ink-bottled soul

a thundering waterfall from timpani

bathing gilt-bronze on bas-relief

new patterns in amplified humanity

pick a snapdragon and three more sprout

when breaths are tissue paper

easily scrunched and ripped

an idea

now *that*

is authored with atoms

UNEARTHING THE UNCONSCIOUS

The night is warm with a breeze that kisses snow to cheeks, melting into hints of jasmine. She dances barefoot, though the grass pokes more than tickles.

They call her witch because she knows her power and has the strength to use it. They call her emotional when she stands her ground, when she won't shrink after hairy troll feet try to squish her garden.

She calls on mother Gaia.

Plucks roses for protection, armor for those she loves, and chamomile for calm, so they can dream and flourish.

Planets pinball through constellations, spattering dust on the universe's roads. And our witch, she must be a witch, gazes up at rainbows to Venus.

She holds out her arm, sturdy as a tree branch. Lustrous black petals brush her cheek in downward stroke before alighting on her shoulder. She gives the raven a coin, and the bird plunges beneath the quilted threads of her garden.

The world slumbers as the black-bill reemerges, bucket clenched in its talons dripping with visions and individuality.

She catches drops in her mug and dips her fingertips. It tastes of books and rejuvenation. She paints the air with lighted swords, taps stars clustered as a marimba, weaves a ballet until the cup is full.

And the jasmine grows a little higher while she counts heartbeats to eternity. The world takes a caffeinated breath. The sun rises.

Feet propped on a new day, raven on her shoulder, she sips her cosmic latte.

HONEY AS DARK MATTER

something rubber-bands us all together

otherwise we'd balloon out

leaving this Earth tilted in dance

the magnolia petals raining into buckets of raspberries

but it's more than pens falling at the speed of flutes

the sea curtsies with pages writ of jewels and starlight

metered verse and rhyming couplets stretched through
time

whispering that you can carry it though you don't see it

growling that you can hunger for it but not eat it

singing that you're imbued with mysterious unseeable
magic

yet we infer it exists, though it's tied with different
strings

by the way a smile can turn into holding wide a door

a shelter of cuddles becomes flexing poses in a mirror

how biting of lips transforms into songbird symphonies

we see the things moved by it—

an invisible giant bending branches—

and we all agree we've metaphorically touched it

though the poets spill words to mop them

hoping to capture the right sequence to explain

and we all agree we've been touched by it

it pulls and it shapes and it endures

THE BREAKING

White horn glistening through the chase

Golden chains wrapped about her waist

Tracked as she flees by marks just there

In soil upturned by hooves in haste

Equine thunder reaches cliffside where

Carousels spin a village faire

Hindlegs crash to crush the crown

Ribbons and childhood in the air

Stamping her hoof, she will not be bound

Pirouettes when the hunt tightens 'round

Transforms limbs to flippers and flukes

Leaps so wonder and dreams will not drown

How To Write A Story

battles on ice with axes

as panthers puff out clouds

lions that talk of old magic

and good that's worth fighting for

daring cliff-side swordfights

as magic spells are knit

and the small, ordinary folk

who do great deeds

princesses in disguise

as asteroids hide scoundrels

rabbits guard the western shores

these words recounted at fireside

an otter strings her bow

as a bard recites poetry

mushrooms make a little girl giant

and grapple with what it means to be human

TASTE

faster than light travel

ship to planet teleportation

shuttles spinning around ring systems

I want a taste

just a taste

nebulas in viewports

holographic interactions

galaxy arms as nightlights

I want a taste

just a taste

replicators and nanites

universal medical devices

the betterment of society

I want a taste

just a taste

The Future is Past

aliens always look like us

the world may have purple sand

but the dominant species is bipedal

a thousand light years away

and we look into a midnight mirror

is it that we lack imagination?

or that we hope to find our best qualities?

in stories, we befriend mermaids

step through portals

and teach others to conquer false gods

we're blank pages — potential to be an odyssey

but instead of cutting off Medusa's head

we write that she's left the frick alone

vampires replace bad blood

instead of sucking the victims dry

we listen to the trees rustling

instead of drowning dryads with chainsaws

the future is past when the world is an orchestra

Once Upon a Time

once upon a time

there was a girl who wanted adventure

she read books about pirates

and about other girls pretending to be boys

so that they could be pirates

and she drew maps and wondered

why did the girls have to pretend?

once upon a time

the girl wanted to swing energy swords

so she did, but they made her prove she was great

when the other guys were just good at it

and she kept achieving new things, doing it on her own

they told her she's so strong but she wondered

why did she have to build those muscles in the first place?

once upon a time

the girl got shimmering stars for making no mistakes

was always told how to fly a little higher

how to make berries just a little bluer, more precise

she planned so much that the space between thoughts

no longer let the fairy dust in and she wondered

why couldn't she be terrible at it and still love it?

once upon a time

a girl decided to believe in her own magic

she turned her hair pink and laughed with mermaids

she dug up the treasure chest that held what she wanted
to be

she wore a flower crown and let fairies tickle her
thoughts

then she wondered

why couldn't she lead an orchestra with her quill

and compose a bigger, better tale?

NAME:
ANCESTRY:
SKILL
INITIAL:
CURRENT:
STAMINA
INITIAL:
CURRENT:
LUCK
INITIAL:
CURRENT:
TALENTS
SPECIAL SKILLS

CIAL CLASS:
DER:
GIC
MAGIC
POINTS
INITIAL:
CURRENT:
ENCE
WEA
1 2 3 4 5 6 7
ARMOUR
1 2 3 4 5 6 7
PROVISION
GP
TREASURE

Myths and Monsters

they look to the sky and see

a wolf eating the light

end times and punishment

bad stuff

I look to the sky and see

the sun tremolo behind the moon's shield

gathering energy

scientists discovering the corona

too faint to see until the light is blocked

good stuff

when they said darkness was evil they lied

they didn't want us to find the truths revealed in shadows

for if we remained fearful of the unseen

we'd never chase the dragons

CONSERVATION OF MASS

131

if matter is neither created

nor destroyed

and love comes from matter arranged in human shapes

then I have loved you forever

and neither supernova nor asteroid collision

will cease my affection

echoing through ley lines of love

and time infinite

STEAMPUNK IT

Cogs turn and the engine trumpets steam. The aeronaut speeds towards another city in the clouds.

She watches the grazing beasts below and the waving hollyhock, and imagines herself nestling in the grass, placing her hands behind her head, gazing up at puffy owls with goggles and airships plunging through them.

A garden to tend and clock hats to craft entirely for accented dimples.

But she has deliveries to complete before coin can leap into her bag. Deliveries can't be automated with horses made of brass and wheels, or mechanical birds as large as an airship.

No, the captains say the best work is done by those capable of ingenuity. As if ingenuity can marimba out of repetition. As if each airship isn't just a line of snare drums marching them into a battle with mundanity.

The aeronaut flies over and above, around and through to another sunrise, tying the sky like a present for someone else to open. Pipes hiss with whispers of another life.

She looks down and wonders if raspberries could paint the right hue for a tailcoat, if the meadow would still be there when her airship was a black and white photograph.

When enough coin was hidden away in her chest with the brass octopus, its tentacles weaving in and out of the container like the slides of a tuba.

Puff, puff, push, push. The ship must sail for the city to float. The city must float for the people to climb. The people must climb to reach what they want.

But what if it all fell?

In her cabin, the aeronaut keeps tiny wheels and springs, tweezers and brushes. She isn't brave enough yet to pop the gasbag and let it screech like a split reed.

Did We Dream the Idea of Space?

did we dream the idea of space?

of wormholes with asteroids sewing

tangled in the galactic chase

did we dream the idea of space?

while leaders on Earth deface

with war, fires, pollution growing

did we dream the idea of space?

for gas clouds fused in allegro pace

weighed by elements slowing

did we dream the idea of space?

of wormholes with asteroids sewing

AGRO FLUCTUATION

I think I'm an indecisive paladin

if I drilled more I could swing more reliably

practiced breaths on hills overlooking ancient lava fields

but some days I prefer the double-bladed axe

going weeks while I ignore the sword

or hesitantly equipping one, then the other

can I wield both?

only to lose interest in them at all

let them hush their clanks as I draw diagrams of mush-
rooms

no interest in blades bashing

pull and repel, magnet opposites

cravings for sriracha on eggs in the morning

and lavender tea in the afternoon

someone whistles "you're up and you're down"

spicy and delicate

solar flare and eclipse

then the light switch plunges it all into "Business Closed!"

why does it feel so in conflict?

don't even mention the times

I grip a staff and summon currents of magic

true, I preferred cutting edges when I was younger

or was it because I was told that's what I had to like?

everyone expects you to stay the same

asks "Why would you even like shields now?"

as if we can't change, evolve

can't carry swords and axes, or nothing at all

figure out who we are at this moment

every day there is a beast to battle

and I don't want to war with myself

LIFE FORCE ON PLANET ETHEREA

Forget not how the east use their power

Or how the Spectres crafted their tower

These crystals in gardens and caves are quite

As versatile and varied as a flower

Warriors fling fire, whip wind into might

Healers mend bone, artificers take flight

The mountain Coils watch and protect them

As the life force within makes dark turn bright

In the west, fear reigns of the witches' gems

The magic they access, religion condemns

But life, all around, is where the power stems

They'd know if they could erase the realms' hems

ARTIFICIAL SOUL

143

humanity is the only animal to create moonlight sonatas

and computers that learn from mistakes

in a world where we are chained to desks

when we're meant to fly

and hopping off moving trucks to collect curdled milk

when we're meant to cultivate gardens

text manipulators arrange the order of words

and call themselves artists

by the images a computer regurgitates

they call themselves authors

by the sentences cut from books and pasted

like we wouldn't see the tape trying to cobble it together

a flood of art made with muddy tools

trying to drown the creatives as it clamors for attention

while I just want AI to do my taxes

and clean my toilet

so I can have more time to bare my soul

to share human experiences and dream with you

about spaceships to tomorrow

TIDES IN THE UNKNOWN

navigating planetary masses

rare landing on powdered surface

visors lifted allowing light to catch

invisible threads between cores

the force of love in gravity

like tides in the unknown

SPACE ELECTRONICA

it's definitely not a particle

the brightness rotating

reflecting light, it's flashing

to the new wave sequence

cosmic drums thump

pumping solar wind through my veins

I moonwalk around the world

with streetlamps for my runway

I'm full of stars, pulsing

in rhythm with the universe

a rocket sforzandos from the atmosphere

I skate on Saturn's rings

harder, better, faster

tilt my cheek toward molecular clouds

whooping at Pluto

something's out there

in a universe of sparkle

listen to its music

the emptiness of space

isn't empty

the emptiness of space

isn't empty

FABLE

Once upon a time

Two seeds were placed in a pot each

Famed was the florist for his marvelous creations

That from far and wide came those intrigued

Among them two who through elations

Claimed to be gardeners of great skill

The florist sold one to a wizard

For he was a hydromancer

Who pledged that the plant would never thirst

And to a second mage, a necromancer

Who swore the plant would never die

But the seedling that never was thirsty

Grew short and thin and pale green

And the wizard demanded the florist take it back

Declaring, "This is the worst plant I have ever seen!"

So the florist put the pot in a macrame sling

The plant that revived even if it died

Produced not a single bud of a flower

And the mage ordered the florist refund her

Shouting, "May your deception turn all your fruit sour!"

So the florist put the pot next door on the cyborg's sill

Then time passed and the two plants grew

With leaves prismatic, large, and glossy

And flowers whose perfume carried for miles

They were planted beneath a tree whose bark was mossy

And the necro and hydro mancers lamented

The florist explained to the water wizard,

"I'd carry the pot everywhere I'd go.

It drank water from streams and lakes,

Rain showers and melted snow.

For though you always gave it water it was still thirsty."

And to the reanimation mage the florist said,

"A cyborg knows one day her parts will fail

So she's kind to all and takes chances

Tries to accomplish so others might spin her tale

For though your plant never died it hadn't lived."

LETTERS TO AGATHA

Dearest Agatha,

My apologies for the bland ink as I've ran out of my favorite glitter. Thank you for your kind suggestion for grounding nettlebriar into powder. I sprinkled it on and around my gladberries, as you instructed, and thus far the pesky gnomes have stopped eating it! As I lay in bed in my camisole (these summer nights are dreadful!) reading Myths and Matcha (do remind me to you tell you why I love it) I can faintly hear zaps and chuckle at the unfortunate gnomes. It serves them right, but do you think I'm being too harsh? Oh, but for autumn to come! Perhaps we can meet somewhere between us both and share a pumpkin roll.

Your friend,

Jade

My Dear Agatha,

How unfortunate that your pegasus delivery was delayed (who ever heard of one losing its wings!). I so look forward to your letters and it pains me to think that you thought I had not written back. But here we are, still writing after all these years. Thank you for sending seeds from your garden. I'm excited to plant them in the spring, mostly so that I can see these red and white painted swirls on the flowers you so beautifully described. My garden will be the envy of the district (if anyone were to pass by, but I'm so far from the main road—as I've undoubtedly mentioned before). Thank you for the reassurances about the gnomes, it is, as you said, no different than pulling up wandering thistle. No long-term damage and they both can find another garden to harass! As for my suggested autumn meet-up, I am very serious. I would not tease you so! What about Lake Sparkle?

Yours truly,

Jade

Darling Agatha,

You must forgive me if I start my letter without acknowledging yours—the gladberries this season are sweeter than sugar fruit! And they have a pleasant aftertaste (I giggle wildly every time). Thank you again for your advice. And for asking about Myths and Matcha. I just finished! It was about a dwarf who'd left his mines to open a tea shop, of all things. Reading it made me feel like drinking hot chocolate while watching the leaves fall. Now, for your silvershroom problem. The best way to rid your garden of the fungus is to harvest it before

the spores fly. You can also boil it into a broth that can be poured anywhere goldengrubs are eating your roots (just keep it away from any critter you want to keep breathing!). It's a shame your husband has you traveling during the harvest season. Perhaps next year?

Affectionately yours,

Jade

My Precious Agatha,

What great misfortune I've read from my letter box! How suddenly your husband was afflicted. I share your sentiments—it is wise to distance yourself so that you do not catch his malady if it is even remotely possible it is contagious. I'll see you at Lake Sparkle in a week (when you read this, that is)! Travel safely and don't forget to pack your goblets!

All my love,

Jade

Restock Needed On Aisle 64bit

running low on RAM

processes failing, lagging

Ctrl-Alt-Delete my day

End Task on laundry

(I forgot it anyway)

Restart the microwave

(my tea went cold. again)

Reminder snoozed on the calendar

(pretty sure "schedule the dentist"

has popped up for a year)

hardware degrading there's a pain in my knee

we can't find the form

I need a Search function in my house

go to Sleep, power down

until someone jiggles the mouse

BEAN BLOSSOM BRIDGE
1880

Pep Talks from Daydreams

Even faeries get dirt on their breeches sometimes. Keep flying.

The princess isn't in the castle. She's catching butterflies with the dragon.

Whenever you think it's a lost cause, imagine you're a pirate with nothing but a compass and a tattered half of a map. Now, hoist your sails. You've got treasure to find.

If you want to live forever, do good magic. Kindness spreads like honeysuckle, it latches on to memory and stories. By these you transcend time, existing in the past and the future.

Lighter-than-air ships weren't built in a day. Why would you solve your problem more quickly? Collect your steam, adjust your cogs, and try again.

The metal is not yet mined that will be forged into the sword that will stop the phoenix from rising.

When the wyvern belches fire, he can still apologize.

Take it from the griffin; you don't have to just be one
thing. Be a lion *and* an eagle.

Don't cut every bloom, or the pixies will have nowhere to
sleep.

Just because harvesting mushrooms by moonlight is easy
for you, it does not diminish its value as a skill. Ask the
werewolf how often he does it.

Still sirens, whose voices mesmerize even on bad days,
can think their own singing sounds flat.

Be emotional, be passionate. Defend your space and cre-
ate inspiration. You aren't an outcast faun, you're a uni-
corn.

Often the princess does the saving, but doing it every day
can be exhausting. Let yourself be rescued occasionally.

True magic is found by loving yourself. It's why magic is
mostly a myth.

NOTES

"Spaceships to Neverland" first appeared in Father 2023 a Poetry Society of Indiana Anthology

"Wishes For My Constellations" first appeared in Mothers 2023 a Poetry Society of Indiana Anthology

"The Breaking", "Waterways of Deceit", and "The Last Centaur" first appeared in The Siren's Song from River City Siren Press September 2024

"Decontamination Station" first appeared in Issue 298 of Aphelion September 2024

"Life Force On Planet Etherea" – Etherea is a planet in the novel Trials of the Innermost, and the Etherea Cycle series. Three realms view magic differently, but their commonality is with the crystals. A Coil, as mentioned in the poem, is a moving settlement of one of the races which guards the crystal caverns. The science fiction and fantasy novel was coauthored by Kristina and her friend Jonathan Fuller.

"Brown County from Space" – This poem was inspired by watching many episodes of Star Trek. Imagine that you are on a ship in orbit and your viewscreen is zooming closer. The many elements and hints of Brown County, Indiana include: en plein air – artists of the early Brown County artist colony used this technical of painting outside of the studio. Neptuning slopes – Brown County is often referred to as the Blue Hills. Jamboree – an annual bluegrass festival started in 1941. Ghost of sundries – Hobnob Corner in downtown used to be a drug store and is now a restaurant. Glass into hummingbirds – refers to the glass blowers in the shops downtown. Forty-six hills – refers to State Road 46 and the hilly terrain. Singing Winds – the name of the House of TC Steele. Fetch a Pail of Water – a reference to the Jack and Jill nut shop in downtown. Daily Grind – name of a coffee house downtown. 16,000 acres – how large the Brown County State Park is. Cheerful coloring - part of the title of a newspaper article "Cheerful Coloring in Indiana Artists' Work," *Indianapolis News*, March 18, 1916. Gnaws a Bone – Gnaw Bone is a community on State Road 46 between Nashville and Columbus. Deer Run – park where softball and soccer are played. The last stanza – a lot has changed since my childhood including a missing gazebo, the restaurant Muddy Boots is no longer there and the addition of Big Woods pizza.

ACKNOWLEDGEMENTS

Many people—whether they know it or not—supported me in creating this book. For a lifetime of support, and everything magical and good in my life, my husband Scott: you celebrated my successes great and small and reminded me to keep dancing under the stars. My far away constellations of writer and creative friends and those who listened to my ideas, your support and encouragement kept me exploring uncharted worlds: Danielle B., JohnWillard U., Jonathan F., Robin Y., Ryan B. . Special thanks to Rue Sparks whose class at the local library on combining words with art, and including me in their writers online group, was the ignition I needed to set my rocket's course to complete this project. Thank you to all my friends, family, and all those who have supported me along the way.

And thank you to my backers of the preorder campaign. Your interest in this project energized me: Danielle Bess, Kristina Southwick, Ryan Benner, Sarah, Robin The Girl Wonder, Diane Billas, Jonathan Fuller, Craig Esser, Cailean Tobin, Dead Fishie, Rae, Megha Baikadi, Aily Enne Bee, Jenny, Jerolyn, Kayla Tuttle, TTRPGkids, Megan R., Melissa, Tina W., The Selkie Delegation

ABOUT THE AUTHOR

KRISTINA W KELLY

Kristina Kelly writes fantasy, sci-fi (often combining the two), and poetry and loves being a geek. Her short stories have received Semi-Finalist and Silver Honorable Mention from the Writers of the Future contest. Kristina's undergraduate pursuits focused on Psychology, Music, and Computer Science. With trumpet as her main instrument and a connection to nature, Kristina often works music and visual landscapes into her writings. Kristina is a trumpet player but dabbles in other instruments, plays video games, and tends to her flower garden and two children.

Kristina currently resides in Indiana with her husband and sons. She is amazed by nature and enjoys painting vivid scenes for her readers. She loves going on new adventures in the great wide somewhere (sometimes just by picking up a new book).

Follow her at www.kristinaeyes.com

facebook.com/kristinawkellyauthor

instagram.com/kristinawkelly

twitter.com/kristinawkelly

tiktok.com/kristinawkelly

goodreads.com/author/show/18116591.Kristina_Kelly

amazon.com/stores/Kristina-Kelly/author/B07DZHBCZZ

youtube.com/@kristinawkelly

ALSO BY KRISTINA KELLY

Thanks for reading! If you liked this book, please consider leaving a review on Amazon and Goodreads.

If you enjoyed the blending of sci-fi and fantasy, explore Etherea in **Trials of the Innermost**. Or it's cozy winter fantasy short story prequel, **The Lady's Crownbearer**.

Tavern Tale, a cozy sapphic fantasy romance with higher stakes set in autumn and inspired by RPGs. What if the side quest is really the main quest?
From www.spacewizardsciencefantasy.com

www.ingramcontent.com/pod-product-compliance
Lightning Source LLC
Chambersburg PA
CBHW042035180726
48295CB00006B/99